ULTIMATE CHALLENGE TIME!

SIMON SPOTLIGHT

An imprint of Simon & Schuster Children's Publishing Division • New York London Toronto Sydney New Delhi
1230 Avenue of the Americas, New York, New York 10020 • This Simon Spotlight edition May 2021
Text by May Nakamura • TM & © 2021 PocketWatch, Inc. & Hour Hand Productions, LLC. All Rights Reserved. Ryan's Mystery Playdate and all related titles, logos, and characters, and the pocket.watch logo, are trademarks of PocketWatch, Inc. All other rights are the property of their respective owners. • Stock photos by iStock

For more information about special discounts for bulk purchases, please contact Simon & Schuster Special Sales at 1-866-506-1949 or business@simonandschuster.com.
Manufactured in the United States of America 0421 LAK
2 4 6 8 10 9 / 5 3 1
ISBN 978-1-5344-8754-3

Hi, I'm Ryan! I'm having a super special playdate today. The only problem is . . . I don't know who is coming to my playdate! Will you help me solve the mystery? We'll be using the stickers in the back of the book to complete three challenges. After each challenge, we'll get a hint about the playdate.

Our first challenge is archery! I have to hit the bull's-eye of three targets. Place the arrow stickers so they hit the center of the targets. Aim carefully!

Did you know? Archery is the national sport in the country of Bhutan.

Bull's-eye!

You have great aim! Now the Mystery Splasher will give us our first hint. Find and place the sticker that fits the shape of the hint.

The hint is a **water bottle**. Hmm, everyone needs water to drink. . . . I think we're going to need more hints to find out about our mystery playdate.

We did it! Now we will receive our second hint. Find and place the sticker that fits the shape of the hint.

The hint is a **sweat suit**. Do you know anyone who likes to wear sweat suits? Maybe my mystery playdate is someone who is always cold.

Let's move on to our third challenge and learn more.

For the second challenge, I'm going to hit this baseball piñata open. **WHAM!**

There's a gold star hiding somewhere among all the balls. Where could it be?

Find the gold star hidden in the picture.

It's a mystery box! The third hint must be hidden inside. But how do we open it? Look! There are red and green buttons on the sides of the box. Try placing the red and green star stickers on the buttons. It might be the trick to opening the box.

Ta-da! The box has a drawer with the third hint inside. Find and place the sticker that fits the shape of the hint.

It is a set of **hand weights**. Wow, they're pretty heavy! I wonder if my playdate is really strong.

The strongest human in the world right now can lift over one thousand pounds!

Let's put all three of our hints together. Place the stickers of the hints onto the Guess-O-Tron screen.

Can you guess who my mystery playdate might be?
Turn the page and find out!

Laurie can swing, jump, and also do a handstand on the bars. She can also jump between two different bars without touching the ground! That must have taken a lot of practice.

Place the sticker of the bar in my hands so I'm swinging from it.

Women's gymnastics has four different Olympic events: vault, uneven bars, balance beam, and floor exercise.

Karlie and I play pirate basketball together. We're on a team against Mommy and Daddy.

Place the basketball sticker in Karlie's hand so she can score a slam dunk. Then place the pirate hat sticker on my head. Arr!

The US women's basketball team has won the Olympic gold medal eight times . . . and counting!

Brandi teaches me how to kick the soccer ball with the side of my foot. I'm going for the goal! Place the soccer ball sticker inside the goal.

The first Olympic women's soccer tournament took place in 1996. The US team won the gold!

It feels so good to play sports and move your body!

I have an idea. Since this playdate was so much fun, I think we should all get gold medals! *Place the gold medal stickers on Laurie, Karlie, Brandi, and me.*

And guess what? For helping me solve my ultimate playdate, you get a gold medal too!

Thank you, and see you again soon!